Goodnight, Mice!

Frances Watts & Judy Watson

ABC
Books

For Noah, Jael and Gabriel – FW

For Oliver Simmons, Katie Petty and Ava Hill-Bione.
And to Dusty, with thanks – JW

 The ABC 'Wave' device and the 'ABC KIDS' device are trademarks of the Australian Broadcasting Corporation and are used under licence by HarperCollins*Publishers* Australia.

First published in hardback in Australia in 2011
Paperback edition published in 2013 by HarperCollins*Children'sBooks*
a division of HarperCollins*Publishers* Australia Pty Limited
ABN 36 009 913 517
harpercollins.com.au

HarperCollins*Publishers*
Level 13, 201 Elizabeth Street, Sydney, NSW 2000, Australia
Unit D1, 63 Apollo Drive, Rosedale, Auckland 0632, New Zealand

National Library of Australia Cataloguing-in-Publication entry:

Watts, Frances.
  Goodnight, mice! / Frances Watts ; illustrator, Judy Watson.
  ISBN: 978 0 7333 3176 3 (pbk.)
  For preschool age.
  Mice–Juvenile fiction.
  Bedtime–Juvenile fiction.
  Watson, Judy.
  Australian Broadcasting Corporation.
A823.4

Designed and typeset by Sandra Nobes
Cover illustration by Judy Watson
Colour reproduction by Graphic Print Group, Adelaide
Printed in China by RR Donnelley on 157gsm Matt Art

16 15 14   18 19

Deep in the forest,
at the base of a tree,
a light is shining...
What could it be?

Peek in a tiny window,
peer through the tiny door,
at the four tiny mice
who are sitting on the floor.

Mitzi is weary and Billy is sleepy.

Clementine's teary and Oliver's weepy.

The mice are too grizzly and tired to play;
it's time to put all the toys away.

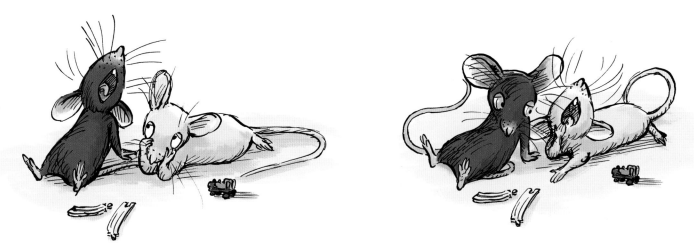

Mitzi yawns once. Billy yawns twice.

Mum and Dad say:
'It's time for bed, mice.'

Grandpa's snuffling,
snoring, snoozing,
a dozy after-dinner nap.

He's woken by a
wriggling, giggling –
four little mice
are on his lap!

Kiss Grandpa once.
Kiss Grandpa twice.

'Goodnight, Grandpa!'
'Sleep tight, mice.'

Rush up the stairs with a jump and a hop –
Mitzi and Billy race to the top.

Climb up the banister,
slide down the rail …
Oliver's falling!
Saved by a tail.

Skittery-skippeting all the way:
now the mice are ready to play!

Mum sighs once.
Dad sighs twice.
What happened to those sleepy mice?

Splish, splash,
and into the tub;
playtime first,
and then we scrub.

Sailing boats, serving tea,
a duck that floats…

a stormy sea!

Wash whiskers once.
Wash whiskers twice.
'Behind our ears, Mum!'
Squeaky clean mice.

When it's Clementine's turn
she's always good;
she sits still and quiet
like a good mouse should.

Oliver says he's nearly grown;
he can do it on his own.
But Oliver's washing ends in tears –
there's soap in his eyes
and his nose and his ears!

Rub-a-dub dry from ears to elbows.
Rub-a-dub dry from tail to tum.

Wrapped in towels
from toes to whiskers...
now the only wet mice
are Dad and Mum!

Toothpaste on chin
and toothpaste on nose,
toothpaste on whiskers
and … Oliver's toes?!

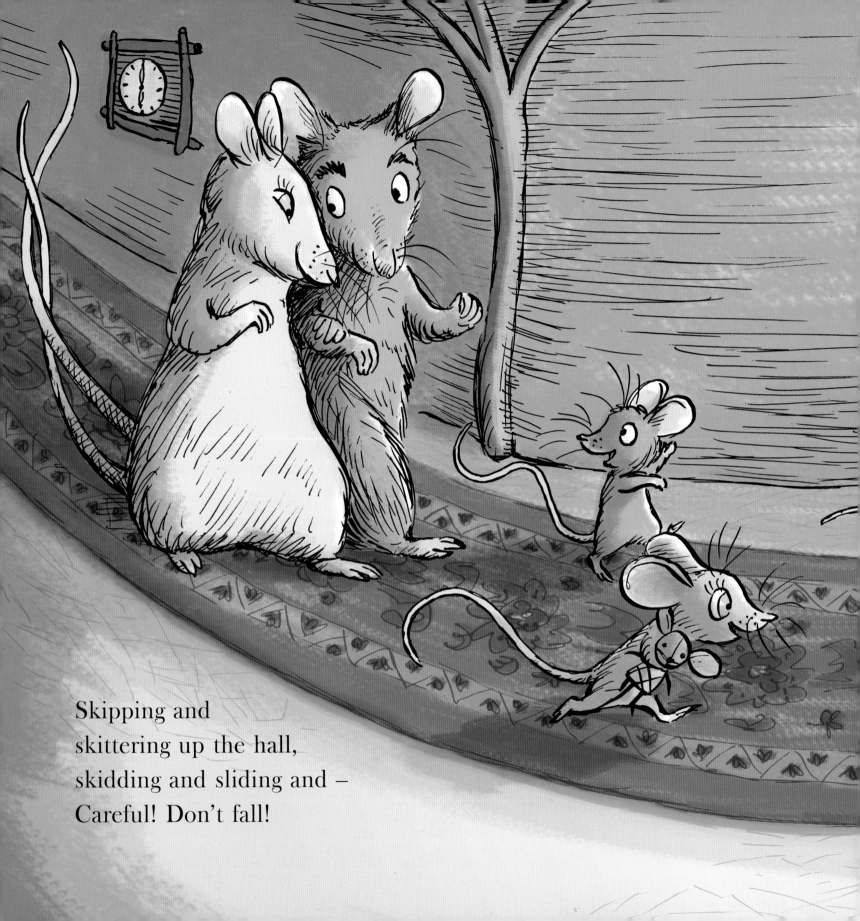

Skipping and
skittering up the hall,
skidding and sliding and –
Careful! Don't fall!

Scampering,
scrambling,
scurrying fun …
so many ways
for mice to run.

'Pyjamas on and then we'll look
for the perfect bedtime book.'

Button up once.
Button up twice.
'You missed a button, Dad!'
Spotty, stripy mice.

'Clementine, Clementine,
where are your whiskers?
Clementine, Clementine,
where is your nose?
I see Clementine's
twitching tail …
I see Clementine's
ticklish toes!'

'I don't *have*
any buttons.'

'Quickly, mice,
hop into bed,
if you want your
story read.'

Read the story once.

Read the story twice.

'Read it again, Dad!'

'That's enough, mice.'

Now heads on pillows and eyes closed tight,
it's time for mice to say goodnight.

Goodnight, Mitzi, with a twitchy-nosed kiss.
Sweet dreams, Billy, with a tight, furry hug.
Goodnight, Clementine, cuddly little miss.
Tuck in baby Oliver, warm and snug.

Turn out the lights and away we creep.
Don't make a sound – not even a peep.
At the base of a tree, in a forest deep,
four little mice are fast asleep.

Goodnight, mice!